Monkey and Elephant and the Babysitting Adventure

Monkey and Elephant and the Babysitting Adventure

Carole Lexa Schaefer

illustrated by Galia Bernstein

CANDLEWICK PRESS

To Monkey and Elephant's
writing adventure best friends:
Liz and Kaylan,
Brenda, Patty, Shellen, and Suzanne,
Christine, Pierr, and Terri
C. L. S.

For Yahli and Roy
G. B.

Text copyright © 2016 by Carole Lexa Schaefer
Illustrations copyright © 2016 by Galia Bernstein

First edition 2016

Library of Congress Catalog Card Number 2015934268
ISBN 978-0-7636-6535-7

16 17 18 19 20 21 LEO 10 9 8 7 6 5 4 3 2 1

Printed in Heshan, Guangdong, China

This book was typeset in Triplex.
The illustrations were created digitally.

Candlewick Press
99 Dover Street
Somerville, Massachusetts 02144

visit us at www.candlewick.com

Contents

Chapter One
A PRIZE

One afternoon, Elephant said, "It sure is quiet around here today."

Monkey wiggled her ears. "Maybe too quiet," she said.

Just then Cousin MeeMee and her babies stopped by.

"Good news!" said MeeMee. "My Mashed Banana Pie won first prize in the Yum-Yum Baking Contest."

"Ooh, that *is* good news," said Monkey, clapping her hands.

"What's the prize?" asked Elephant.

"A cartful of coconuts," said MeeMee.

"Nice!" said Monkey.

"Yes," said MeeMee. "But I must pick them up at Tasty Cooking School—too far to take my babies."

"Not too far for me," said Baby One.

"Not far for me," said Baby Two.

"Not me, tee-hee," said Baby Three.

"If only I had a babysitter," said Cousin MeeMee.

Monkey looked at Elephant.

"It really is too quiet around here," she said. "We will babysit for you, MeeMee."

"We *will*?" said Elephant.

"Of course we will," said Monkey. "Right, Elephant?" She gave him a little poke.

"Um," said Elephant, "of course."

"Oh, thank you, Monkey and Elephant," said Cousin MeeMee. "I'll bring the babies over tomorrow after breakfast."

"Mmm, I like breakfast," said Baby One.

"Mmm, and lunch," said Baby Two.

"Mmm, and snacks, tee-hee," said Baby Three.

MeeMee and the babies waved
bye-bye and headed for home.

"Um, Monkey," said Elephant,
"have you ever babysat before?"
Monkey shrugged. "No, not
really. Have you?"

"No, never," said Elephant.

"Well, then, best friend," said
Monkey, "here we go again—
together on another adventure!"

Chapter Two
SOME RULES

"Monkey," said Elephant the next morning, "do you think babysitting will be hard?"

Monkey scampered up his trunk and settled behind one big ear.

"For babysitting," she said, "we need some rules."

"What rules?" asked Elephant.

Monkey scratched her head and looked down the path.

"I will tell you when I know," she said, scrambling down Elephant's trunk. "They're here!"

"We want to *play*!"
shouted Baby One.
"Play with *you*!"
shouted Baby Two.
"Play with *me*! Tee-hee,"
shouted Baby Three.

MeeMee blew kisses
and hurried away.
The babies ran
around Elephant.

They grabbed his tail, squeezed
his ears, and jumped rope with his
trunk.

"Ouch!" cried Elephant.

"Rule Number 1," said Monkey.
"Play—but not too rough. Okay?"
"Okay," they all agreed.

"I want to race now!" hollered Baby One.

"Race fast!" shouted Baby Two.

"Race *me*, tee-hee," squealed Baby Three.

"No, me! Me! Me!" they all shouted.

"Quiet, please!" said Monkey.
"Rule Number 2: No Me, Me, Me."
She drew a line in the dust.

"Everyone starts here at the
same time. Okay?"
"Okay," the babies agreed.

"Now listen for Elephant's trumpet," said Monkey.

Wha-wha-whaa! Elephant blew. "Go!"

The babies raced back and forth, back and forth, until . . .

"Too *hot*," said Baby One.

"Give me WAH-TER," said Baby Two.

"I *HUNGRY*," said Baby Three, without a tee-hee.

"Uh-oh," said Elephant, "are they whining?"

"I think so," said Monkey.

"Is there a rule for it?"

Monkey held up three fingers. "Rule Number 3: Snack now, nap later."

Elephant set down cups of water. Monkey gave the babies some banana chips.

They nibbled and yawned, nibbled and yawned.

"And when you finish eating," said Monkey, "it's nap time."

But by then, they were already snuggled up asleep.

Ahuha, Elephant yawned. "Babysitting sure is hard work."

Monkey closed her eyes. "Yes, it sure is."

Chapter Three
HOME AGAIN

Rustle. Rustle. Rustle.

In the tall dry grass, three riff-raff wildcats crouched low and whispered, "Did you know that monkeys are a very good snack?"

"Did you know that *baby* monkeys are the very *best* snack?"

"Oh, oh, oh—I see THREE of them right now!"

Elephant sniffed. "I smell riff-
raff wildcats," he said.

Monkey opened her eyes. "Me,
too," she said. "What'll we do?"

"Make **Rule Number 4**," he told
her. "Always keep babies safe."

"Look," hissed one riffraff wildcat. "Now there are *four* monkey snacks."

"And one BIG elephant!" yowled another.

"YIKES!" they screeched, running away fast.

"And stay away!" snorted Elephant.

The babies woke up. They
rubbed their eyes and looked
around.

"I see Elephant right by me,"
said Baby One.

"I see Monkey," said Baby Two.

"I see *Mommy*, tee-hee-hee," squealed Baby Three.

"Hello, hello, hello," said Cousin MeeMee. "What did you do while I was gone?"

"Played **Not Too Rough**," said Baby One.

"And **No Me, Me, Me**," said Baby Two.

"And **Snack, Then Nap**, tee-hee," said Baby Three.

"Sounds nice and busy," said MeeMee.

"Where's your prize?" asked Elephant.

Cousin MeeMee pulled a cart full of coconuts out of the tall grass.

"Here," she said. She put a big pile of coconuts in the grass.

"For you, good babysitters," she said.

"Thanks!" said Monkey and Elephant.

"Ooh!" yelled Baby One, running toward the cart. "Room for babies to ride. Me first!"

"No, me!" said Baby Two.

"Me, me! Tee-hee!" said Baby Three.

"*Ahem,*" said Elephant.

"Uh-oh. **Rule Number 2**," said Baby One.

"**No Me, Me, Me**," said Baby Two.

"Sorry, tee-hee," said Baby Three. They helped one another into the cart.

"MeeMee," said Elephant, "even though you have a cart now, *sometimes* can we still babysit?"

"So things won't get *too* quiet?" said Monkey.

"What do *you* say, babies?" asked MeeMee.

"Sometimes? For sure! *WHEEE*—tee-hee!" they agreed, and waved bye-bye.

Monkey and Elephant sat in the shade sipping fresh coconut juice.

"Ahh," sighed Monkey. "A nice way to end this adventure."

"Mmm, adventure," said Elephant.

"What we both like," said Monkey. "Right, friend?"

"Just right," said Elephant, "for our Very Own Rule: Monkey and Elephant will stay ADVENTURE friends —"

"And BEST friends," added Monkey.

"FOREVER!" Monkey and Elephant promised together.